For my lovely Mum,
and for my Dad, whose wonderful
bedtime stories taught me to believe in magic!

My mum and dad

Sky Pony Press books may be purchased in bulk at special discounts for sales promotion,
corporate gifts, fund-raising, or educational purposes.
Special editions can also be created to specifications. For details, contact the Special Sales Department,
Sky Pony Press, 307 West 36th Street, 11th Floor, New York, NY 10018 or info@skyhorsepublishing.com.
Sky Pony® is a registered trademark of Skyhorse Publishing, Inc.®, a Delaware corporation.
Visit our website at www.skyponypress.com.

10 9 8 7 6 5 4 3 2 1

Manufactured in China, November 2013
This product conforms to CPSIA 2008
Library of Congress Cataloging-in-Publication Data is available on file. ISBN: 978-1-62873-590-1

Ellie
and the truth about the
Tooth Fairy

Jules Miller

Sky Pony Press
New York

Daily News

Tooth Fairy leaves yet another coin!

Another child hides a tooth and finds a coin under pillow.

Dogs prove to be way more clever than we thought

BEST BRUSH EVER

One day a girl named Ellie, from a town not far from you,
had a plan to prove the Tooth Fairy couldn't possibly be true!

She told her best friend,
"Wait and see. I'm going to find the truth.
I'm going to trick the grown-ups
with a teeny, tiny tooth."

But the clever mom of Ellie's friend (who'd overheard the plan)
made a very urgent phone call, saying,
"Help me if you can!"

At bedtime Ellie hid her tooth
but didn't tell her mom.
Soon she'd really know
the truth if the fairy didn't come.

She shut her eyes but didn't sleep,
laying quietly with her toys.
She listened up for "goings on"
and general fairy noise.

Then at twelve o'clock (or there about),
when the world was fast asleep,
a fairy woke up Ellie, saying,
"I've heard that we should meet."

"Ellie, can you come with me,
there's a place I'd like to share,"
explained the lady dressed in white
with lovely auburn hair.

In no time at all (they flew quite fast), they reached some silver gates.

"Quick, quick!" cried the fairy. "There's lots to see and little time to waste."

They hurried up a pearly path toward a castle with a moat,
where they crossed a toothpaste river in a pretty paper boat.

The fairy then unlocked the door
with a shiny golden key,
and flying on ahead she said,
"Come in and follow me."

For every child there is a space – for every tooth there is a place

Daisy

what? why? How? How? Why? Why? what? what? How? why?

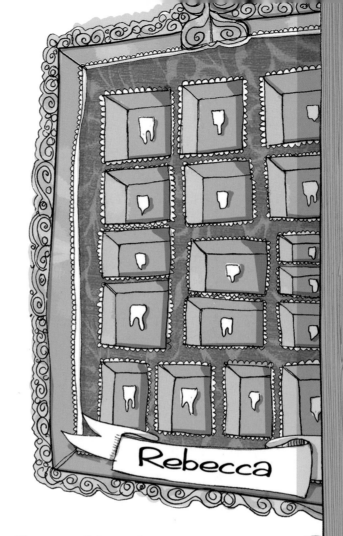

Inside a long white hallway hung a million golden frames
filled with trillions of tiny teeth and inscribed with children's names.
Ellie wondered How? and Why? and What was it all for?
So many questions filled her head that they tumbled to the floor.

For every child there is a space – for every tooth there is a place

"This is where all teeth end up;
for every tooth there is a place,
and every time a child is born,
we make another space."

"And these, dear Ellie, are all your teeth, placed in a golden frame,

Ellie

and underneath—as you can see—we've written in your name."

"Now, moving on," the fairy cried,
"there's plenty more to see!

There are **retired fairies cleaning teeth** and our famous Peppermint Tree."

The next stop a clearing in the woods,
where nothing goes to waste.
"It's here," the fairy pointed out,
"that we make our Peppermint Paste."

The Golden
Toothbrush Tree

"And this room's where the toothbrushes grow,"
the little fairy told.
"They're for very special children
and are made of fairy gold!"

But there was more on this fairy tour, and they flew both high and low until a clock chimed half past one and it was time for them to go.

"Now, close your eyes," the fairy said,
"and you'll wake up in your bed.
You'll not remember very much,
but think you've dreamed instead."

So when Ellie woke and found a coin where her tiny tooth had been,

she had to wonder to herself:

Had it all been just a dream?

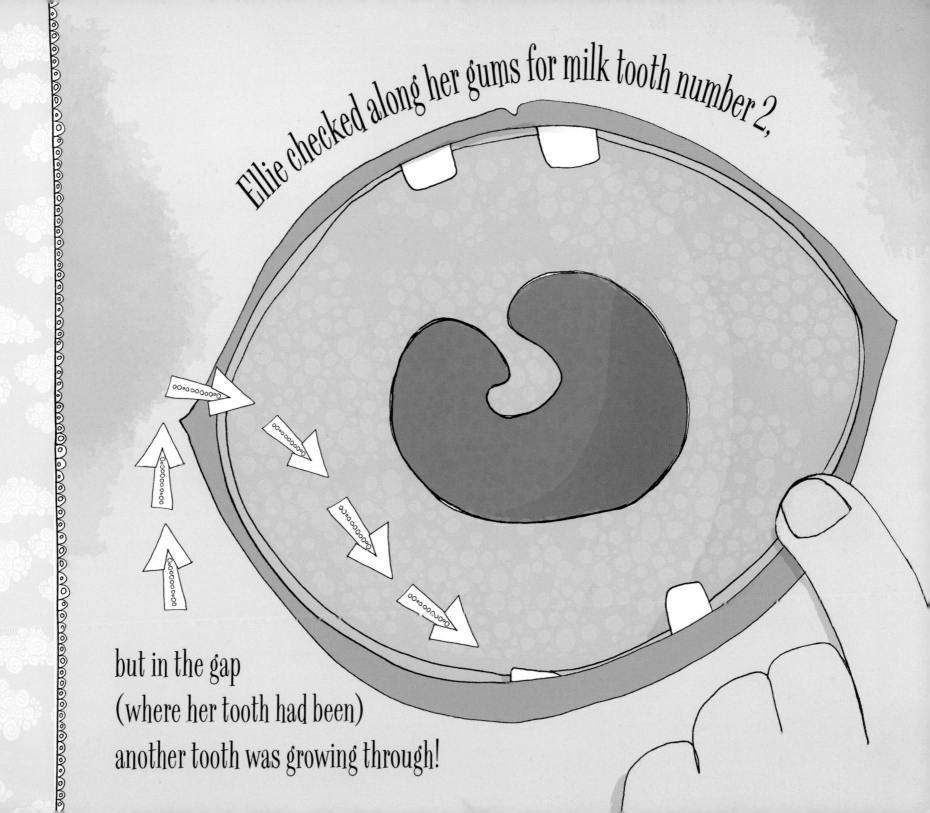

Ellie checked along her gums for milk tooth number 2,

but in the gap
(where her tooth had been)
another tooth was growing through!

Just then her mom knocked on her door, saying,

"Something special's just arrived!
Open this up right away.
It could be a nice surprise!"

So that morning while her mommy watched, Ellie did unwrap the truth
when she found a Golden Toothbrush to clean her brand-new shiny tooth.

Now, we both know who sent the box
(and that secret's safe with us),

but please remember your tiny teeth,
and don't forget to brush!